Smallest Brownie and the Flying Squirrel

Smallest Brownie and
the Flying Squirrel

by Gladys L. Adshead

pictures by Richard Lebenson

New York   Henry Z. Walck, Inc.

Library of Congress Cataloging in Publication Data

Adshead, Gladys L
  Smallest Brownie and the flying
squirrel.

  SUMMARY: When Flying Squirrel tries
to look after a curious little Brownie,
they both get into trouble.

[1. Fairy tales] I. Lebenson, Richard,
illus. II. Title.
PZ8.A23SK   813'.5'4 [E] 72-3202

ISBN 0-8098-1195-2

To Ninnette and Alec and that flying squirrel

Smallest Brownie was curled up in a cosy corner under the root of an apple tree. He was having a little snooze.

The other brownies were off about their own affairs. They had forgotten that at LEAST one brownie should always look after Smallest Brownie.

Flying Squirrel slept all day and went about at night. He had very big eyes, made for night seeing. He would curl his flat furry tail around himself like a blanket when he slept. An extra piece of skin on each side of his body

It was nearly twilight, between daytime and night-time. Flying Squirrel often watched the brownies when he was awake. Very soon he would be gliding into the night. He was furry and soft and the brownies sometimes snuggled up to him.

stretched from front to back legs. When he glided from place to place the skin spread out like a sail.

Smallest Brownie wakened. He rubbed his eyes and looked around. Not a brownie was in sight. Flying Squirrel was watching Smallest Brownie. His big eyes could see him very well.

The sun had just set. The clouds were changing color from pink and gold to gray and purple. A flock of birds flew by. Smallest Brownie watched them going home for the night. The crickets began to chirp in the grass. A little breeze blew up. It was all very lovely and Smallest

Brownie began to think what he would do at such a beautiful time.

Smallest Brownie jiggled on his toes. Flying Squirrel glided to a lower branch of the tree. Smallest Brownie's long ears heard the little sound even though Flying Squirrel's glide was soft as velvet.

"Hello, Flying Squirrel, are you going somewhere?"
asked Smallest Brownie.

"I always go places at twilight," said Flying Squirrel, "and in the nighttime as well."

"I'm going somewhere too," Smallest Brownie said, suddenly making up his mind what he would do. "I'm going to the house of Old Grandmother and Old Grandfather."

And off he went skippity-hop, skippity-hop.

Flying Squirrel knew the brownies should be looking
after Smallest Brownie, but they were nowhere to be seen.
He decided HE had better look after Smallest Brownie, so
he glided over the roof of the house, looked over the edge

of the gutter, and watched to see what Smallest Brownie would do.

Old Grandmother and Old Grandfather had been out in the lovely twilight watching the birds go home and

listening to the crickets chirping. They were just going back in the house when Smallest Brownie arrived. Before they closed the door, Smallest Brownie slipped inside.

Old Grandmother and Old Grandfather did not see him.

Flying Squirrel could not go through the door because it was shut. So he crawled up the roof to the chimney, up the stones with his claws, and down inside the

chimney. Fortunately, there was no fire in the fireplace.

Old Grandfather sat down and turned on the lamp beside his chair. Old Grandmother sat down in her chair and turned on the lamp. She took out her knitting and

began to knit some socks for Old Grandfather. Old Grandfather picked up a book and began to read to Old Grandmother.

Flying Squirrel sat on the mantelpiece and watched them, but he could not see Smallest Brownie. "Where is Smallest Brownie?" he wondered.

Smallest Brownie had hidden himself, but he was watching Old Grandmother and Old Grandfather. He thought they looked very comfortable and nice sitting in

their chairs under the lamplight. He did not know Flying Squirrel had come into the house too.

Flying Squirrel was anxious. He knew Smallest Brownie should be safe at home. He knew Smallest Brownie was in the house. Where COULD he be?

Flying Squirrel looked at the top of the curtains. Perhaps the curtain rod would give him a better view.

He glided silently to it and clutched the rod with his feet and claws. He peered over the top but he still could not see Smallest Brownie. He decided to scramble down the inside of the curtain and look for Smallest Brownie from the floor.

"I heard a little sound," said Old Grandmother. "What do you suppose it was, Old Grandfather?"

"I didn't hear any little sound," Old Grandfather replied, looking up from his book. "It must be your imagination, Old Grandmother," and he went on reading.

Old Grandmother counted the stitches on her needle.

At the sound of their voices, Flying Squirrel had scrambled up the inside of the curtain and peered over the rod again. Smallest Brownie's long ears heard the little sound. He crept out from under a chair and waved to Flying Squirrel.

Now Flying Squirrel knew where Smallest Brownie had been hiding. But how was he going to get him home?

He began to climb down the curtain again. The curtain moved—just a little—wherever Flying Squirrel's body was.

Old Grandmother put down her knitting. She had heard the little sound again. She saw the curtain move— just a little. "Old Grandfather," she said, "SOMETHING is behind the curtain. Perhaps it is a mouse."

Old Grandfather put down the book and crept

QUIETLY over to the curtain. He put his hand gently but SUDDENLY over the little bulge he saw and GRABBED.

But Flying Squirrel was too quick for him. Up he ran and there he was again, peering over the curtain rod.

Smallest Brownie put his hands over his mouth and giggled.

"Well!" exclaimed Old Grandfather. "That little bulge was too big to be a mouse. I wonder whether it could

be a flying squirrel. I wish I could have caught it to put it outdoors, so it would be happy."

"Perhaps we will find him sleeping in some corner tomorrow morning," said Old Grandmother.

"I hope so," Old Grandfather replied. "I wonder where he is now."

Smallest Brownie giggled again. Flying Squirrel's huge eyes were looking down from the curtain rod.

Smallest Brownie was so interested that he was now quite near Old Grandfather.

Old Grandfather stepped back. He ALMOST stepped on Smallest Brownie. Smallest Brownie scuttled

away in a hurry and hid behind the frill at the bottom of the couch.

Flying Squirrel was learning that looking after Smallest Brownie had its complications. Smallest Brownie

had disappeared again. "Where IS that little brownie," wondered Flying Squirrel. "How am I ever going to get him home?"

Flying Squirrel silently glided to the mantelpiece. He made a small scuttering sound which only Smallest Brownie's long ears heard.

By this time Smallest Brownie was getting tired of hiding. He decided to go home. BUT the door was shut. Smallest Brownie sat down to think. "How can I make someone open the door?" he wondered. "And how will Flying Squirrel get out of the house?"

"Old Grandmother thought there was a mouse," he said to himself. "I'll pretend to be a mouse." He began to make a lot of little scrabbling sounds. But that did not draw anyone's attention. Then he used his fists tap-tapping on the door.

"What ARE those little sounds on the door?" said Old Grandmother. "Something must be outside wanting to come in. You had better look, Old Grandfather."

"Perhaps it is the neighbor's cat," Old Grandfather replied, putting down his book. "You had better get a saucer of milk ready, Old Grandmother. That's why it likes to come in."

Old Grandmother went into the kitchen. Old

Grandfather went to the door. Smallest Brownie squeezed himself into the corner near the edge of the door. Flying Squirrel saw from his high lookout place what was about to happen. Just as the door opened and Smallest Brownie

rushed out, Flying Squirrel took off in an ENORMOUS
glide through the air and was out over Old Grandfather's
head in a twinkling.

Old Grandmother came from the kitchen. "Here, kitty, kitty, kitty," she said.

"There is no cat," said Old Grandfather. "Perhaps it was only branches rubbing against the door."

They looked all around the room again for Flying Squirrel. They could not see a sign of him, nor did they hear any sound. "I wonder whether he glided out of the house when I opened the door," Old Grandfather said. Once more they settled down to their knitting and reading.

"Where am I?" Smallest Brownie said as he ran through the dark night. All the light had faded from the

sky. "I wish I were home, I wish I had big eyes to see in the dark like Flying Squirrel, I wish Biggest Brownie and Middle-Size Brownie would come to find me. Oh, dear,

I wish the sun had not gone away. I wish there was a big full moon."

Meanwhile, Biggest Brownie, Middle-Size Brownie and the others had come home. They missed Smallest

Brownie. "Where is Smallest Brownie? Has anyone seen him lately?" Biggest Brownie cried.

All the brownies shook their heads. "We must look for him at ONCE," they said.

They began to hunt, here, there, everywhere. They kept very close together because it was so dark.

Flying Squirrel had glided into the top of a high tree.
Now was the time to get Smallest Brownie safely home.
He heard Smallest Brownie sobbing and saw him sitting
under a bush with tears rolling down his cheeks.

"Smallest Brownie," said Flying Squirrel gliding down beside him, "climb on my back and I will take you home."

Smallest Brownie was VERY glad to see Flying Squirrel. He rubbed the tears away with the back of his hand, sniffed a very big sniff, and climbed onto the soft, furry back of Flying Squirrel.

Flying Squirrel took off, his sailing skin spread out. In no time at all he glided down among the surprised brownies. Smallest Brownie clambered down.

"Oh, Flying Squirrel, you found Smallest Brownie!" they exclaimed.

"Where HAVE YOU BEEN, Smallest Brownie?" asked Biggest Brownie.

"I went into Old Grandmother's and Old Grandfather's house, BUT THEY DIDN'T SEE ME," replied Smallest Brownie.

"I saw him go," explained Flying Squirrel, "so I followed him to bring him home."

"Thank you, thank you Flying Squirrel, oh, THANK YOU VERY MUCH," said all the brownies.

Middle-Size Brownie hugged Smallest Brownie.

Then Smallest Brownie smiled a big smile, rubbed his face on Flying Squirrel's soft fur, and gave him a big hug.

"Thank you for rescuing me, Flying Squirrel," said Smallest Brownie. "You are my good friend."

About the Author

Gladys L. Adshead was born in England and attended college in London. She came to the United States in 1921 to do social work in Baltimore, where she established the first open-air nursery school on a pier at the harbor side. She soon took up teaching in elementary schools and established a reputation as a popular storyteller both in libraries and for private groups. She has taught in schools all over the country and spent some years as headmistress of a private school outside Boston. Miss Adshead now lives in New Hampshire.

About the Artist

Richard Lebenson attended high school in New York and received his art training at the Pratt Institute, Brooklyn. In 1965 he was chosen to be one of eight participants in a special summer training program organized by Hallmark Cards. His work has been exhibited in various parts of the United States and in England. Mr. Lebenson, who lives in Brooklyn, has illustrated many books for children, including *Caspar and his Friends* by Hans Baumann and *The Witch's Brat* by Rosemary Sutcliff, as well as Gladys L. Adshead's *Brownies—They're Moving!*

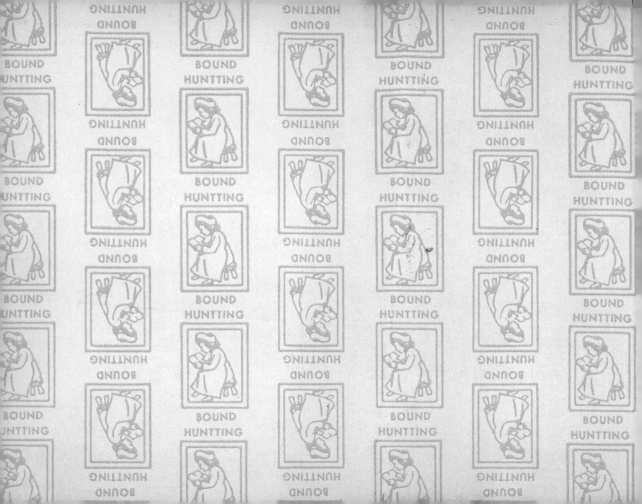